APRIL-2-81P-0.5

Tame and Wild

by Alison Auch

Content and Reading Adviser: Joan Stewart
Educational Consultant/Literacy Specialist
New York Public Schools

Spyglass
BOOKS

COMPASS POINT BOOKS

Minneapolis, Minnesota

Compass Point Books
3722 West 50th Street, #115
Minneapolis, MN 55410

Visit Compass Point Books on the Internet at *www.compasspointbooks.com*
or e-mail your request to *custserv@compasspointbooks.com*

Photographs ©:
Two Coyote Studios/Mary Walker Foley, cover (cat in basket); PhotoDisc, cover (wildcats); PhotoDisc, 4; Visuals Unlimited/Jim Whitmer, 5 (senior and child); Visuals Unlimited/Mark E. Gibson, 5 (family reading, family in front of houses); PhotoDisc, 6, 7; Visuals Unlimited/Gregg Otto, 8; Visuals Unlimited/Tom J. Ulrich, 9; PhotoDisc, 10, 11, 12, 13, 14; Two Coyote Studios/Mary Walker Foley, 15; Visuals Unlimited/Daphne Kinzler, 16; Visuals Unlimited/Joe McDonald, 17; Two Coyote Studios/Mary Walker Foley, 18; Corel, 19; PhotoDisc, 21.

Project Manager: Rebecca Weber McEwen
Editor: Jennifer Waters
Photo Researcher: Jennifer Waters
Photo Selectors: Rebecca Weber McEwen and Jennifer Waters
Designer: Mary Walker Foley

Library of Congress Cataloging-in-Publication Data

Auch, Alison.
  Tame and wild / by Alison Auch.
    p. cm. -- (Spyglass books)
Includes bibliographical references (p.   ).
Summary: Brief text compares and contrasts domestic and wild animals of
the same family, such as cats and lions, guinea pigs and voles, and hogs
and wild boars.
  ISBN 0-7565-0226-8 (hardcover)
  1. Domestic animals--Juvenile literature. 2. Animals--Juvenile
literature. [1. Domestic animals. 2. Animals.] I. Title. II. Series.
  SF75.5 .A88 2002
  636--dc21
                        2001007380

Contents

Families

Most people belong to
some kind of a family.
Besides our own family,
all people are enough alike
that we are part of
one huge family.

Animals belong to
big families, too!

Cats and Lions

House cats are fast and have very strong jaws. They are good hunters, which makes them like their relatives...

... *Lions*! Lions are also good hunters. They hunt deer, zebras, and antelope for their food.

Fun Facts
Cats usually weigh 6 to 15 pounds (3 to 7 kilograms). Lions can weigh up to 500 pounds (227 kilograms).

Guinea Pigs and Voles

Guinea pigs are shy animals that make good pets. They eat plants and *grains*. Their diet is one thing that makes them like their relatives...

... *Voles*! Voles mainly eat plants. Voles are shy animals that often live underground.

Fun Facts

Guinea pigs can be 8 to 14 inches (20 to 36 centimeters) long. Voles are usually about 5 inches (13 centimeters) long.

Cattle and Yaks

Cattle usually live on ranches or farms. They eat grass. Their diet is one thing that makes them like their relatives...

... *Yaks!* Wild yaks eat grass and other plants. Wild yaks are big, **bold** animals. They can slide down icy slopes and swim across rivers.

Fun Facts
Cattle can weigh more than 2,000 pounds (907 kilograms)! Wild yaks can weigh up to 1,200 pounds (544 kilograms).

Horses and Zebras

Horses are smart, strong, and fast. Their speed is one thing that makes them like their relatives...

... *Zebras!* Zebras can run 40 miles (65 kilometers) per hour. They are hunted by lions and cheetahs. They need to be fast!

Fun Facts

Horses can weigh more than 1,000 pounds (454 kilograms). Zebras can weigh up to 600 pounds (272 kilograms).

Hogs and Boars

Hogs, or pigs, *wallow* in mud to cool down. Wallowing is one thing that makes them like their relatives...

... *Boars*! Wild boars also wallow in mud to cool down. They are strong and some have thick *tusks* for fighting.

Fun Facts

Hogs can weigh up to 500 pounds (227 kilograms). Wild boars weigh up to 400 pounds (181 kilograms).

Rabbits and Hares

Rabbits have very strong
back legs for hopping.
Their legs are one thing
that make them like
their relatives...

... *Hares!* Snowshoe hares also have powerful back legs. Their fur turns white during winter. This **camouflage** keeps them safe.

Fun Facts

Rabbits usually weigh from 2 to 11 pounds (1 to 5 kilograms). Snowshoe hares weigh about 3 pounds (just over 1 kilogram).

Dogs and Wolves

Dogs make good pets. They don't like to be alone. Their need for company is one thing that makes them like their relatives...

... *Wolves!* Wolves also like to be around each other. In the wild, they live in groups called packs.

Fun Facts

Dogs can weigh from 6 to 200 pounds (3 to 91 kilograms). Wolves can weigh up to 120 pounds (54 kilograms).

Invent Your Own Animal

The *tame* and wild animal relatives in this book often look like each other.

1. Think of a wild animal you didn't find in this book. Imagine how it would look if it were a tame pet. Draw it!

2. Now, write about how it would be different from its wild cousin.

Glossary

bold—brave and unafraid

camouflage—behavior or appearance that lets something hide in its surroundings as a protection from danger

grains—seeds from plants such as grasses

tame—something that is not wild, and often lives with humans

tusks—long, thick teeth that stick out of an animal's mouth

wallow—to roll around in the mud

Learn More

Books

Hewitt, Sally. *All Kinds of Animals*. New York: Children's Press, 1998.

Threadgall, Colin. *Animal Families*. New York: Crown Publishers, 1996.

Young, Dianne. *A World of Difference*. Vancouver/Toronto: Whitecap Books, 1999.

Web Site

Cool Science
www.hhmi.org/coolscience/critters/ index.html

Index

GR: G
Word Count: 306

From Alison Auch

Reading and writing are my favorite things to do. When I'm not reading or writing, I like to hike in the mountains or play with my five cats!